STEPHEN J. GROA

Illustration by Soon Kwong Te

CHRISTMAS YVE

A Kiwi elf's dream to join Santa

Christmas Yve
A Kiwi Elf's Dream to Join Santa

v3.0

Illustrated by Kwong Teo

Bible verses quoted from the King James Version by World Bible Publishers, Inc. "Only begotten Son": KJV John 3:16. "Let not your heart be troubled": KJV John 14:1. Copyright registration #TXu1- 950 - 771

Outskirts Press, Inc.
http://www.outskirtspress.com

ISBN: 978-1-4787-6673-5

PRINTED IN THE UNITED STATES OF AMERICA

Dedicated to all the Sunday school students who have graced my class and animated my Christmas plays. A sincere thanks to my wife, Teresa (and her ears), as I tinkered with the lyrical qualities of the text, and to Michelle for giving Yve her initial form. Tiffanie, June, Barbara, Michael, and Roger (St. Nick) also have a special place in my heart. Ta.

This Book Belongs to:

____

MULBERRY ST

’Tis a little known fact that elves share our globe.
They adorn our planet like a queen and her robe.
Why, there are elves in Scotland, elves in Spain,
Elves in Mexico, Turkey, and the hamlets of Maine.

They’re right under our noses, they’re in the next room;
They’re friends of our parents, part of the baby boom.
Go out and greet them, shake hands should you meet
In drives, crescents, roads—on Mulberry Street.

Whatever your ***lingua***, whatever your ***franca***
(Your mum gave me that word; go ask her and thank her)
Elf, elfe, manó, dwende—they all mean the same:
A mystical small creature who’s good at their game.

Somewhere at this moment, right here, right now,
There are elves making tacos, elves milking cows,
Elves eating mangoes, elves playing the flute,
Elves picking cherimoyas and kiwifruit.

There are elves playing rugby, elves watching the telly,
Elves hitting baseballs and making mint jelly,
Elves putting on the kettle for a cup of tea,
Elves enjoying test cricket at the MCG.

Now close your eyes and sit real still,
And quiet the mind as part of your drill.
Listen—to the right, they're humming and singing,
And whispering and whistling, and ring-a-ding-dinging.

In any discussion, if most elves are being Frank—
Not Elsie, not Waldo, not Mildred, nor Hank—
They eventually reveal where they most want to be:
At St. Nicholas's workshop and his Grand Christmas Tree.

PEACE

CHEERFULNESS

GOODWILL

JOY

Making presents for children, with barely a breather,
From blueprints of cheerfulness floating in the ether.
For the meek and the merciful, courageous and bold,
The sweet and the innocent, the young and the old.

Assembling peace by peace with joy and goodwill
Trinkets and toys and gifts with great skill;
In all shapes and sizes, in red, white, and blue,
Rhombuses, trapeziums—to name but a few.

Far, far from the North Pole, way, way down yonder—
Don't attempt it by foot; it's too far to wander—
Past Mongolia and Thailand and the Timor Sea,
Past Rockhampton, Toowoomba, Tamworth, and Sydney.

Once you hit Tassie, make a sharp left turn,
To the land of the Kiwi, and the mighty silver fern,
Aotearoa, New Zealand, Land of the Long White Cloud,
With Māori and Pakeha: a people quietly proud.

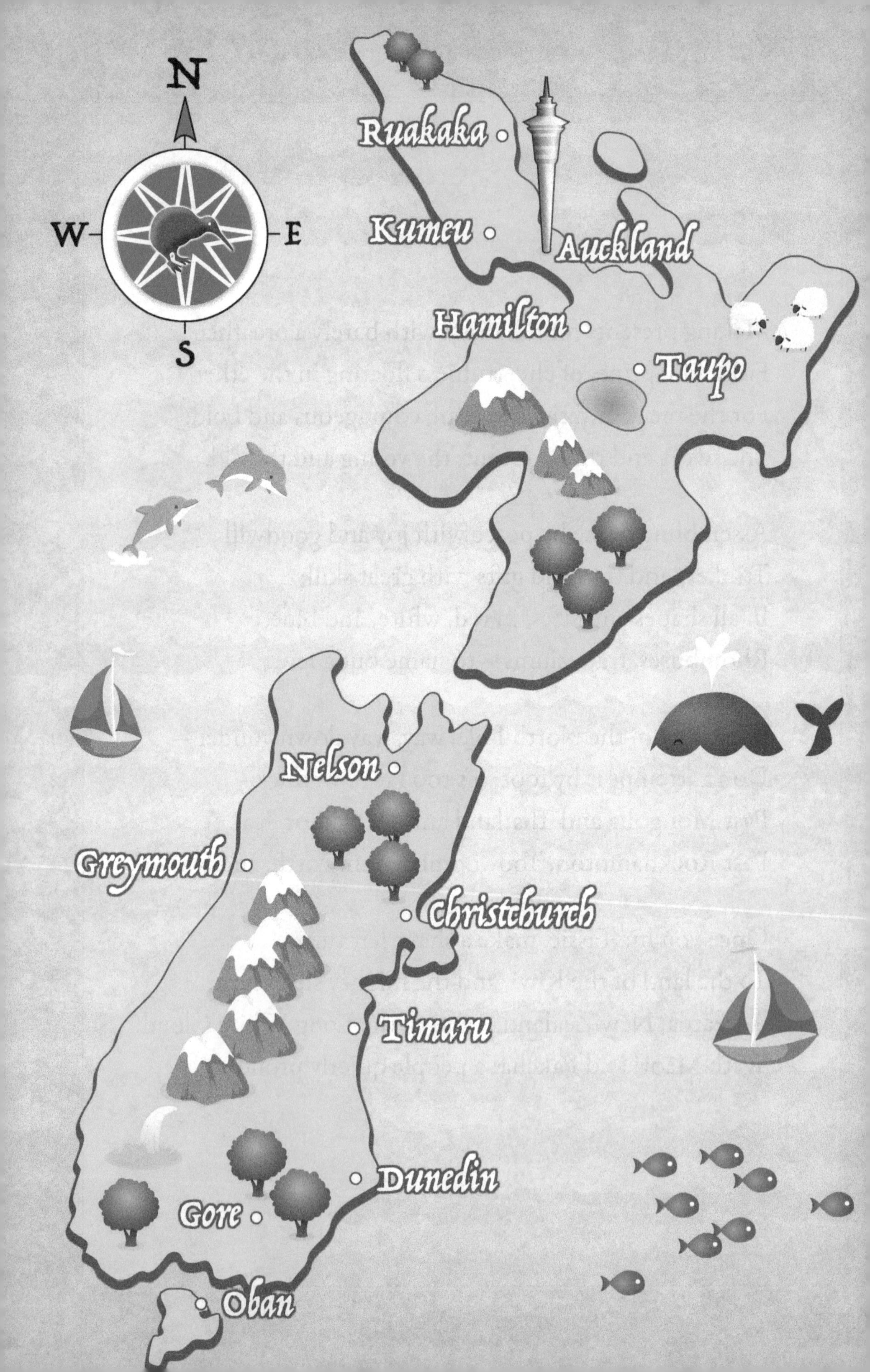
N
W
E
S
Ruakaka
Kumeu
Auckland
Hamilton
Taupo
Nelson
Greymouth
Christchurch
Timaru
Dunedin
Gore
Oban

Past Ruakaka, Kumeu, and the suburb of Kelston,
Past Hamilton, Taupo, and the city of Nelson,
Past Greymouth, and Timaru, Dunedin and Gore.
Hang in there, I beg you, there's not much more.

Slow down, you passed it, the Island of Stewart.
If you land on Antarctica, sorry, mate, you blew it.
Back up, back up: latitude forty-seven degrees south,
For here begins our tale, from this reindeer's mouth.

In the town of Oban lived an elf named Yvette.
(Note: her best mates called her Yve, lest I forget.)
Her days were spent swimming, hiking, and playing;
Her evenings, after supper, on her knees praying.

The great wish of her heart, of her mind, of her soul,
Was to join St. Nick's team at the frosty North Pole.
But how does an elfish lass follow her dream?
With a smoldering passion, and a will full of steam.

SANTA CLAUS
NORTH POLE
HO-HO-HO

Now some try to contact Santa by text, fax, or mail;
The latter includes both the "e" and the snail.
Of course, when writing a letter, begin with "hello,"
And don't forget the post code of HO-HO-HO.

Yve did all of the above, four score and ten.
She was busy with phone, busy with pen.
She also took comfort that once every year,
St. Nick flew overhead with his eight reindeer.

She had an intuitive sense that Santa's keen vision
Could read every heart with insightful precision,
So she composed and broadcast feelings of goodwill,
Waiting for her time, and her dreams to fulfill.

For to Yve's way of thinking, Santa Claus was a saint,
More than a white beard, red suit—oh, so quaint—
But a servant to Him without equal, bar none,
The Christ in Christmas: the "only Begotten Son."

Lastly, each year on the twenty-fourth of December
(It's also Yve's birthday; that's how I remember)
In the sand of a cove, she'd write with purpose and nerve,
HELLO, SANTA; READY TO SERVE!

I'll see you at midnight
atop the magical tree,
I'll swoop down from above
a'coming for thee.

Then, then it happened—a response in a wave,
As Yve sat quietly inside a seaside cave.
As the water receded into the ocean,
Gone was her message in the ensuing motion.

Now on the beach clearly written in the sand
Was a message from Santa's far-reaching hand:
I'LL SEE YOU AT MIDNIGHT ATOP THE MAGICAL TREE,
I'LL SWOOP DOWN FROM ABOVE A-COMING FOR THEE.

Yve bounced up and down; she flipped forward and back.
She did handstands and cartwheels and a jumping jack.
She cried, "My time has arrived, my time to head north,
My time to realize the effort I put forth."

Suddenly the hop skipped out of Yve's jump
As it quickly dawned on her with quite a thump
That she had crawled every cranny, explored every nook,
Hiked every hilltop and swam every brook.

But never ever, never ever, never—that's five!—
In her walks, in her strolls, in her afternoon drives,
Had she encountered this tree with the faculty of her senses.
Not in backyards, nor behind neighbourhood fences.

But time was running out, not a second to lose.
Yve packed her toothbrush, jacket, and shiny red shoes.
She searched hither and thither; Lord only knows,
In the boots of cars, between a hedgehog's toes.

One o'clock, two o'clock, three o'clock, four,
Five o'clock, six o'clock, seven, and more.
T minus sixty—time was running out.
She was frazzled and dazzled, running all about.

A minute to go—not a second to lose.
Would Yve make it? What would she choose?
I will struggle and strive 'til my time runs out.
Never surrender; never give in to doubt.

In the calm that thought brought, in the still of the night,
She became aware of a glowing, glorious white light.
It came from the forest—a fair distance it seemed.
It glowed, it radiated, shone and gleamed.

To this beacon she sprinted, off to the races,
Away with the sorrows of sad, somber faces.
Yve ran into the woods, past bushes and vines,
Past flowers and ferns and flora and pines.

To Yve
from St. Nick

She went deep, and then deeper, and then deeper still,
Powered by resolve and a growing sense of thrill.
And then in the stillness, in the quiet, in the calm,
She saw a majestic sight worthy of a psalm.

Dead center in the forest, in living red and green,
Was the most bonny pohutukawa tree Yve had ever seen.
At the top of its trunk was a five-pointed star;
You could see it from near, you could see it from far.

On its branches hung ornaments, candy canes, and bells,
Framed photos of eight reindeer, glass balls, and shells.
Strings of lights, snow globes, ribbons and bows,
Figurines of angels with golden halos.

At its base—a Nativity Scene of crystallized comet dust.
An eternal reminder of a Divine living trust
That refuge is here: "Let not your heart be troubled,"
But enlivened, strengthened, buoyed, and humbled.

Also, a wrapped gift labeled *"To Yve from St. Nick."*
She tore off the paper and gave it a flick.
Revealed were red gumboots lined with sheep's wool.
Yve slipped them on gracefully with barely a pull.

Up she bolted seven branches, skyward bound,
Intrigued and delighted as the tree buzzed with sounds;
A symphony of music—flutes, harps, and gongs,
Whistles and warbles and tinkles and bongs.

Her toes starting tingling, her knees began knocking;
A warmth in her belly, her tonsils a-rocking.
Her heart slowed down, skipping three beats.
In the air was the aroma of sugary sweets.

Just seconds to go...fifty-eight, fifty-nine,
But where is Santa? Please give Yve a sign.
Failure now and she'll feel like a chump.
Wait...in the heavens—a message: jump!

The stars had aligned; the command was so clear.
With a heart full of faith, she leapt in the air.
As the reindeer swooped down, Santa extended his hand.
He caught Yve midair; she was part of his band.

Off they shot, nearing the speed of light,
Encircling the globe all through the night,
Bringing gifts to kids wherever they called home,
Including Bogota, Pretoria, Mumbai, and Rome.

Just outside Newcastle, the sleigh skidded on ice.
It spun round and round, not once but thrice.
Santa, the reindeer, Yve were all dizzy,
Bamboozled, transfroozled, woozy, and frizzy.

Danger, o' danger—all might be lost!
As they scooted along in the snow and the frost,
For barreling down from an adjacent road
Was a gimungous lorry, carrying a full load.

They twirled out of control on the ice and the sleet.
Someone needed to step up and think on their feet,
To slow down and halt Santa's speeding sleigh
Before disaster befell this Christmas Day.

Yve was ready to honour a Māori legend of ol'
And be like Rakiura—assume its role.
The island had been the anchor stone of Māui's canoe
As he fished up Te Ika-a-Māui along with his crew.

With a roar of defiance from this tiny, brave elf,
Yve leaned behind Santa's sleigh, asserting herself.
Stamping her gumboots, she gave a hard stomp
Again and again—BOMP, BOMP, BOMP.

She dug in her heels, providing resistance—
Deeper, then deeper with compounding persistence.
She was gaining a foothold, ploughing a trail.
With a sprinkle of grace, they just might prevail.

The sleigh slowed down, petering to a halt.
As the lorry rumbled by, giving all a jolt,
The driver was shocked when Santa he saw.
He was gobsmacked, startled, down fell his jaw.

Santa offered a wave and then off they flew;
No more drama that night, to their task they stayed true.
All presents delivered, every one on the list,
So, back to the North Pole, relax, a game of whist.

For Yve's act of valour, Santa took her aside.
Smiling with joy and beaming with pride,
He said, "***I want you on my team, so be ready, my dear.***
Henceforth, you will join us on the twenty-fourth of each year."

Yve's response was immediate, his hand she did take,
And with firmness of purpose, gave it a shake.
So, now every Christmas Yve anchors Santa's flight
As they travel the globe, delivering gifts through the night.

The End

CPSIA information can be obtained
at www.ICGtesting.com
Printed in the USA
BVHW010153201219
567247BV00021BA/4/P